# Dear Parent:

Congratulations! Your child is taking the first steps on an exciting journey. The destination? Independent reading!

**STEP INTO READING®** will help your child get there. The program offers five steps to reading success. Each step includes fun stories and colorful art. There are also Step into Reading Sticker Books, Step into Reading Math Readers, Step into Reading Write-In Readers, Step into Reading Phonics Readers, and Step into Reading Phonics First Steps! Boxed Sets—a complete literacy program with something for every child.

## Learning to Read, Step by Step!

**Ready to Read** **Preschool–Kindergarten**
• big type and easy words • rhyme and rhythm • picture clues
For children who know the alphabet and are eager to begin reading.

**Reading with Help** **Preschool–Grade 1**
• basic vocabulary • short sentences • simple stories
For children who recognize familiar words and sound out new words with help.

**Reading on Your Own** **Grades 1–3**
• engaging characters • easy-to-follow plots • popular topics
For children who are ready to read on their own.

**Reading Paragraphs** **Grades 2–3**
• challenging vocabulary • short paragraphs • exciting stories
For newly independent readers who read simple sentences with confidence.

**Ready for Chap**ters
• chapters • longer
For children who w chapter books but still like colorful pictures.

**STEP INTO READING®** is designed to give every child a successful reading experience. The grade levels are only guides. Children can progress through the steps at their own speed, developing confidence in their reading, no matter what their grade.

Remember, a lifetime love of reading starts with a single step!

Published in the United States by Random House Children's Books, a division of Random House, Inc., New York, and simultaneously in Canada by Random House of Canada Limited, Toronto. No part of this book may be reproduced or copied in any form without permission from the copyright owner.

www.stepintoreading.com
www.barbie.com
Educators and librarians, for a variety of teaching tools, visit us at
www.randomhouse.com/teachers

Library of Congress Cataloging-in-Publication Data
Jordan, Apple.
On your toes / by Apple Jordan ; illustrated by Karen Wolcott. — 1st ed.
    p.   cm. — (Step into reading. Step 1) "Barbie."   SUMMARY: Barbie and Kelly look at photographs of Barbie's ballet performances.
ISBN 0-375-83142-8 (trade) — ISBN 0-375-93142-2 (lib. bdg.)
[1. Ballet—Fiction.   2. Photographs—Fiction.   3. Dolls—Fiction.]
I. Wolcott, Karen, ill.   II. Title.   III. Series. PZ7.J755On   2005   [E]—dc22   2004005599

Printed in the United States of America  First Edition  10 9 8 7 6 5 4 3 2

STEP INTO READING, RANDOM HOUSE, and the Random House colophon are registered trademarks of Random House, Inc.

# STEP INTO READING

**STEP 1**

# Barbie™
# On Your Toes

by Apple Jordan

illustrated by Karen Wolcott

Random House New York

# Barbie loves to dance!

She loves to leap.

# She loves to jump.

She loves to spin.

And she loves
all the costumes!

"Do you like one best?"
Kelly asks.

Barbie is not sure.

She opens her album. . . .

Barbie is a princess.

She wears a pink tutu.

Her prince wakes her
with a kiss!

Barbie is a good swan.

She wears a white gown.

She is a bad swan, too.

She wears all black.

Barbie is a fairy

with a golden crown.

She dances with candy
canes and cookies.

# Barbie is a magic bird.

She flies and flutters
on her toes.

Barbie is a puppet
who comes to life.

She bends and moves
as if she is on strings.

"I love all my costumes,"
says Barbie.

"But I love to dance
no matter what I wear!"

"Me too!" says Kelly.